READ
THIS
BOOK IF
YOUDON'T
WANT A
STORY

t

e

f   s   o   b

To Lani and Mckayla, my loves

R.P.

To dear friends, Kevin Barrett and family

E.Z.

TILBURY HOUSE PUBLISHERS

12 Starr Street
Thomaston, Maine 04861
800-582-1899
tilburyhouse.com

Text © 2019 by Richard Phillips
Illustrations © 2019 by Eric Zelz

Hardcover ISBN 978-0-88448-705-0
eBook ISBN 9780884487074

First hardcover printing September 2019

2 4 6 8 10 9 7 5 3 1

Library of Congress Control Number: 2019940801

Scanning and color balancing by Alan LaVallee, Visual Art Imaging, Thomaston, Maine
Printed in China through Four Colour Print Group, Louisville, KY

Designed by Eric Zelz
Illustrations were done in gouache and pastel on Arches 300 lb. hot press paper.
The text type is Goudy Old Style.

elves

ducks

pickle

fuzzy

laughter

READ THIS BOOK IF YOU DON'T WANT A STORY

STORY BY RICHARD PHILLIPS

PICTURES BY ERIC ZELZ

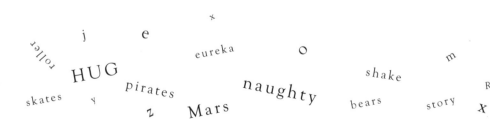

T he Book With No Story is the name of this book.
No elves that are naughty, no pirates with hooks.
No frogs become princes, no dogs driving cars.
No rockets on journeys to Saturn or Mars.
I'll show you no pictures, no scares and no thrills,
no cows on trapezes, no fish with big gills,
no polar bears on snowboards, no quacking duck bills ...

b

j

z

Hello?

Um. Excuse me.
How can a book have no story?

Who said that?

Page 6.
Look up in the top
left corner.

Well, Page 6, because I am
The Book With No Story,
and I should know.
The Book With No Story
is me, and I alone decide
whether or not I tell a story.

Now, where was I?
Ah yes ...
No polar bears on snowboards,
no quacking duck bills,
no cyclists on high wires,
no acrobat skills. No bears that
are fuzzy, no genies gone bald,
because The Book With
No Story is what I am called.
No once upon a times,
no happily ever afters,
no roller-skating llamas
to induce laughter.
No uplifting ending when
the beginning was sad.
No story at all. Period.
Too bad ...

Shouldn't I have some
say about this too?

Who's asking?

Page 8.
Hi, and welcome to my
cool page. Do you like it?

What is going on here?

I agree with Page 6. Every book needs a story.

I don't care, Page 10. I will not tell a story! And anyway, we've turned the page on Page 6. It's history!

Listen to me Pages 1 through 11. I will have no story and I mean it!
I'm the book and I say what kind of story to tell.

Ah—ha! You said "story."

I made a mistake.

No you didn't.

Yes I did, Page 12!

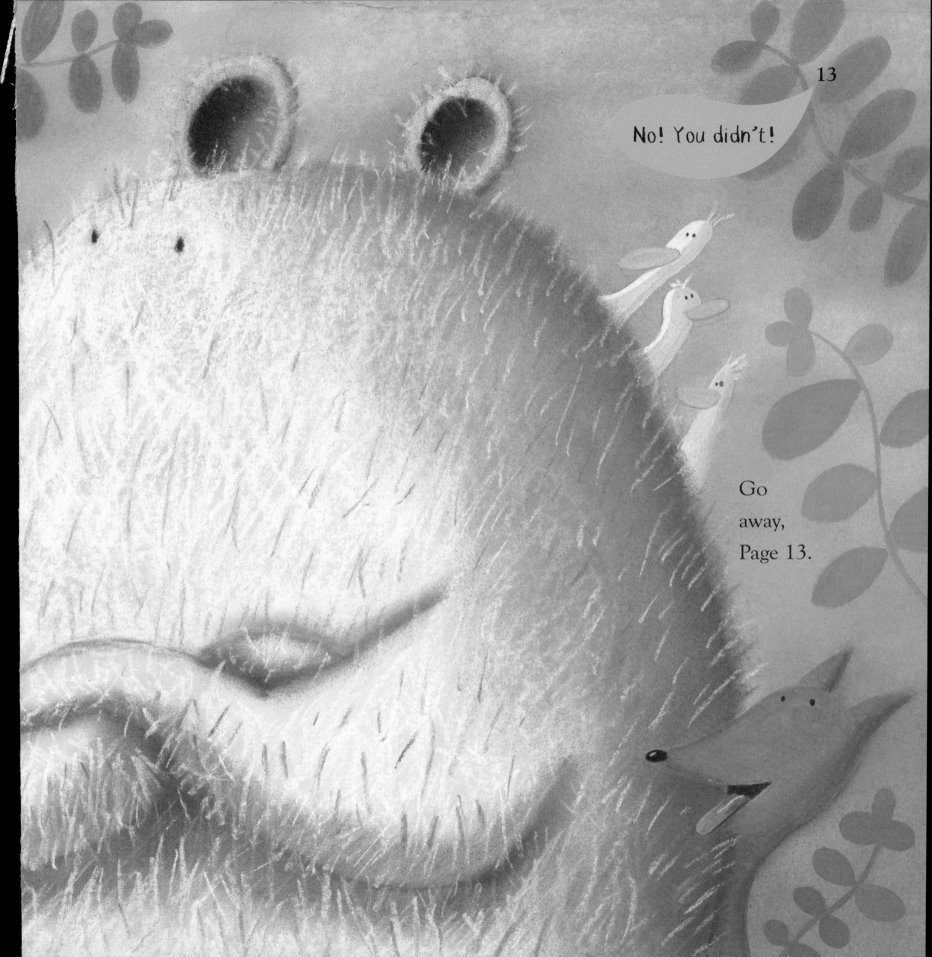

May we ask why you don't want to tell a story, Mr. Book?

Because I just don't!

But what's the point of a book with no story? Don't you want the reader to be entertained?

For the last time, No!

For the last time, why not?

v

a

o

c

n

r

m

Because, maybe,
I just don't have
a story to tell. OK?
Now are you satisfied?

Aw, come on, Mr. Book!
We can help you tell a
GREAT STORY!
Go for it, Page 16!

RETURN TO SENDER

RETURN TO SENDER

t   b   n   v

p

We just wanted to inspire you with a supercool opening!

I don't want to be inspired, Page 17! I just want to be a book with no story, and especially without a Giant Woolly Tundra Snail, whatever that is.

Now leave me alone!

22

Shake!
Shake!
Shake!

Ahh...that's better. Thank you, Reader. Now, Mr. Book, the words seem to be pouring out of you! How do you feel?

frogs   dogs   pirates   thrills

Mars

story

magic

I can breathe again, but I think my pages have come loose.

Trust us, Mr. Book, your pages have been loose for a long time. Ready to tell a story?

I guess so. But I'm still afraid I don't have anything interesting to tell.

Well, you'll never know if you don't try.

elves

fish

story

snowboards

duck

roller skates

Okay...here goes.

Once upon a time, there was a book
who felt he had no story to tell.
But then his annoying pages gave him
a hug and talked his readers into shaking
his words loose and told the book he
was capable of telling a story.
THE END.
How was that?

Meh...

Meh?

We think you
can do better.

Better?

There's
magic
in you,
Mr. Book.
You just have
to let
it out.

25.

Okay... Let me think.

EUREKA!

I have an idea! Why don't we all create stories with the words we already have!

I'll start.

Once
upon a
time there
was a timid
book who
thought he had
nothing to say,
and then ...

A book full of stories
is what I've become.
Imagine a story and
let's have some fun!
Imagine a poem.
Imagine a play.
But don't ever imagine
you have nothing to say.

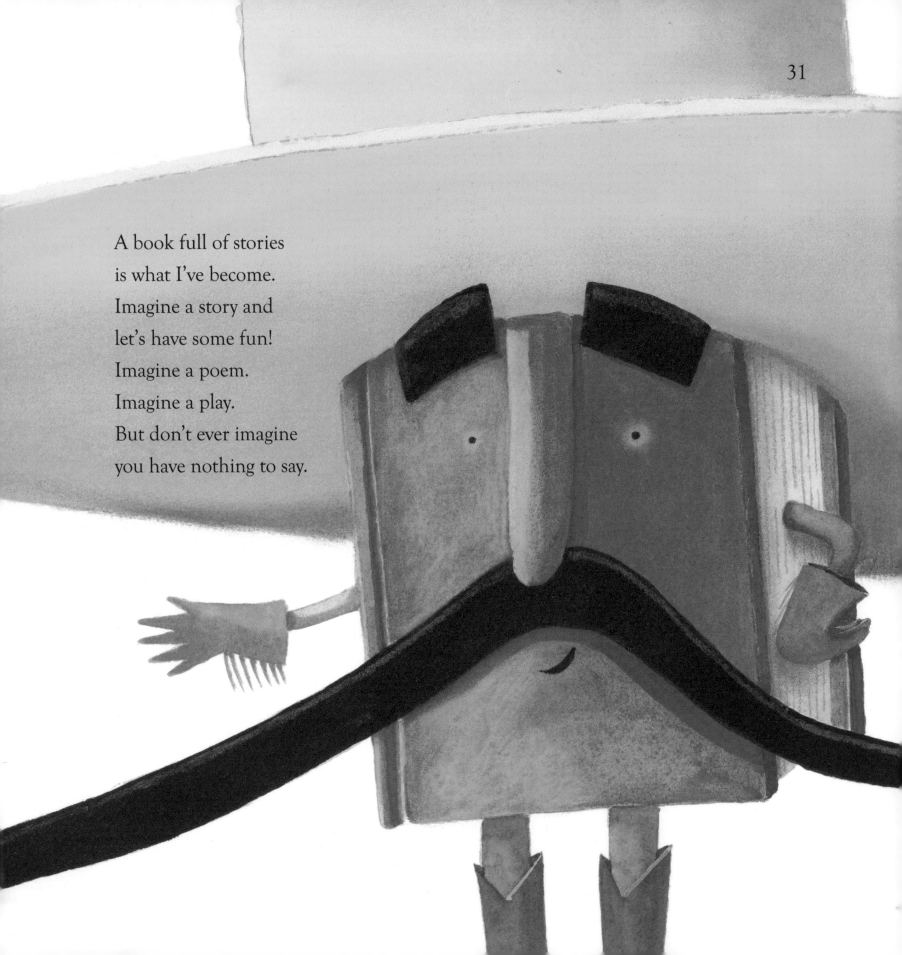

RICHARD PHILLIPS was born in a hospital in Washington D.C. He was 18 inches tall and weighed 7.4 pounds. Since then, he has grown 5 feet taller, gained 179 pounds, written 2 feature films, a TV show on PBS, an award-winning animation series, 8 children's books, 24 screenplays, and 5 TV pilots. His first film, *EDEN*, won 14 awards including the "Audience Award" at the SXSW Film Festival. Richard lives in Maryland with his wife, Lani, and daughter, Mckayla, who inspired this book by challenging her dad to write a book with no story.

ERIC ZELZ was immediately intrigued when invited to illustrate a book with no story. Would it be a lot of work, or none at all? Eric's illustration, design, and journalistic work has been recognized by organizations including the Society of Environmental Journalists and the Society for News Design. He is also the illustrator of *Pass The Pandowdy, Please* (National Council for the Social Studies/Children's Book Council Notable Social Studies book). See more of Eric's work at **ericzelz.com.** Eric lives in Maine with his wife, Abby, and daughter, Charlotte.